THE MAN
WAS THE MOON

MIKE RUSSELL

Published by StrangeBooks.

www.strangebooks.com

Cover designed by the author.

StrangeBooks receiver & transmitter maintainer:

Jay Snelling

ISBN: 9798718262308

www.strangebooks.com

for all who love the moon
and for all who do not

THE MAN WHOSE WIFE WAS THE MOON

1969, June 29th:

The moon was full in the night sky above America.

In Washington DC, in Rock Creek Park, on top of a hill, sat a small, circular pool of water; upon the surface of the water, filling it perfectly, was the full moon reflected.

Dressed in a black cloak, an eighty-four-year-old woman with long, white hair, walked through Rock Creek Park, between the trees, then up the hill and stood facing the pool. She looked down at the reflection of the moon and smiled, then she looked up at the moon and bowed.

The woman reached her left hand beneath her cloak and withdrew a small, empty, glass bottle, sealed with a glass stopper. With her right hand, she removed the stopper. She then knelt down and reached her left hand through and beyond the moon's reflection, fully submerging the bottle and holding it under. Bubbles rose from beneath the surface of the water and burst from the reflection's craters. When the bubbles ceased, the woman lifted the bottle out of the pool and the rupture she had made in the moon's reflection closed up. The water on the outside of the bottle dripped back into the centre of the pool, causing ripples to spread across the reflection's craters and expand to its circumference. The pool then reverted to stillness, its surface resuming its undistorted mirroring.

The woman returned the stopper to the bottle, then returned the bottle beneath her cloak. She raised herself to standing, looked down at the reflection of the moon and smiled, then looked up at the moon and bowed. Still bowing, she walked backwards down the hill, then turned around, raised her head and walked away from the briefly disturbed reflection of the continuously undisturbed moon.

Earlier that same day, in a Washington DC junior high school, uniformed students with impassive expressions filed into a large assembly hall. They organised themselves into orderly rows, facing a stage at the end of the hall. Upon the stage, stood Principal Brannigan, a large man with a stern expression, close-cropped, grey hair, a large, grey moustache, and wearing a dark grey suit. Standing next to him was an upright pole, from which hung the American flag. On the floor in front of him was a slide projector. On the wall behind him was a large projection screen.

'Attention!' Principal Brannigan shouted.

The students all obediently stood up straight.

'Sit!' Principal Brannigan shouted.

The students all obediently sat on the floor.

'We have a guest speaker,' Principal Brannigan said with his characteristic unnecessary aggression. 'He is an astronomer. He is here to teach you about the moon.'

Principal Brannigan marched off the stage, then marched past the seated students, to the back of the hall, where he stood to attention, with his back to the wall, his eyes constantly moving from side to side, scanning the students for misdemeanours.

A twenty-eight-year-old man, wearing a brown corduroy suit, ambled onto the stage. He ran his hands through his unkempt, shoulder-length, brown hair and brown beard, straightened his brown necktie, then stood in the centre of the stage, facing the students, and smiled.

The students all looked back at the man with impassive expressions.

'Hi,' the man said. 'My name is Arthur Hart. I have two loves: my wife and the moon.'

Arthur walked to the side of the stage, flicked a switch on the wall and the room darkened. He walked back to the centre of the stage, flicked a switch on the slide projector and on the screen behind him there appeared a projected photograph of the full moon.

11

'This is the first photograph I ever took of the moon,' Arthur said. 'Isn't she beautiful? Isn't she extraordinary? I have many more photographs of her to show you. Some of them are highly detailed and reveal parts of her that have only ever been seen by a very small number of people.'

He paused.

'But there is an aspect of the moon that cannot be photographed; an aspect of the moon that cannot be seen with even the most advanced telescopes. And that is what I am here to talk about. You may have noticed that I refer to the moon as *she* and *her.* That is because I am here to talk about the moon as a subject, not an object.'

The students all continued to gaze at Arthur with impassive expressions. At the back of the hall, Principal Brannigan furrowed his brow, narrowed his eyes and peered at Arthur suspiciously.

'Why do I use *feminine* pronouns?' Arthur said. 'Because the moon embodies the feminine; just as the sun embodies the masculine. Let me clarify what I mean by *the feminine* and *the masculine.* I am not talking about gender. I am not talking about sexuality. I am talking about the fundamental principles that exist within us all, regardless of our gender or our sexuality. Every

12

one of us has both the masculine and the feminine principles within us.'

At the back of the hall, Principal Brannigan mumbled, 'Utter nonsense,' whilst simultaneously making a mental note to grow his moustache a little longer.

Arthur continued:

'Within some of us, the masculine principle is more dominant; within some of us, the feminine principle is more dominant. But both exist within us all. The feminine principle that exists within us all is receptive, sensitive, intuitive, creative... Various cultures in different places and different times have recognised these qualities in the moon and expressed them in myths which describe the aspect of the moon that cannot be photographed, the aspect of her that is beyond the physical, the aspect of her that I call, to the disgust of my colleagues, the spirit of the moon.'

At the back of the room, Principal Brannigan's mouth fell open.

'In this lecture I will be sharing with you a selection of these myths. They are not to be taken literally but nor are they to be dismissed, for they express very eloquently the moon's extraordinary nature, her power, her mystery and her significance, and in studying them we can regain that which in our society we have lost. It

13

is my sincere hope that this lecture will inspire you to view the moon afresh, to view her with awe, with reverence and with wonder, and show you that she is more than just a rock.'

Principal Brannigan inadvertently let out a guffaw. Arthur ignored it and continued:

'Let us begin with the myth of the moon goddess Selene who rode a silver chariot across the sky, pulled by white horses...'

Arthur went on to describe numerous moon myths from around the world and throughout history, whilst at the back of the hall, Principal Brannigan shook his head and glowered at Arthur with furious disdain.

1969, June 30th:

As the sun rose, a twenty-eight-year-old woman with long, dark hair, wearing a white T-shirt and blue bell-bottomed trousers, walked through downtown Washington DC towards a small bungalow on J Street, then knocked on the door.

The door opened, revealing an eighty-four-year-old woman with long, white hair, dressed in a black cloak. The older woman peered at the younger woman and said:

'Your name is Molly.'

The younger woman smiled with delighted surprise.

'Yes,' she said. 'How do you know that?'

'You are planning to give a speech for us all.'

'Yes,' Molly said, still smiling.

'And you want something to help you express what needs to be expressed.'

'Yes,' Molly said.

The woman with long, white hair reached her left hand beneath her cloak and withdrew a small, glass bottle, which was filled with water and sealed with a glass stopper.

'It lasts for twenty-eight days,' she said as she handed the bottle to Molly.

'Thank you,' Molly said.

The woman with long, white hair smiled, then shut the door.

In a Baltimore junior high school, Arthur Hart stood on another stage, in another hall, facing another assembly of students. He was wearing the same brown corduroy suit as before. There was a slide projector on the floor in front of him and a large projection screen on the wall behind him. He ran his hands through his brown hair and beard, straightened his brown necktie, and smiled.

The students all looked back at Arthur with impassive expressions.

Arthur began, once again, to recite his lecture:

'Hi. My name is Arthur Hart. I have two loves: my wife and the moon.'

Whilst Arthur's lecture continued, far away, in Washington DC, Molly removed the stopper from the glass bottle, put its rim to her lips and drank.

Arthur suddenly felt confused. He put his hand to his head.

'Where was I?' he said with a frown.

He stared imploringly at the front row of seated students.

'Where was I?' he repeated, more urgently.

'You said you have two loves,' one of the students called out.

'Two?' Arthur said. 'No, no, no. I don't have two loves. I have only one love.'

He put his hand to his head again.

'I'm very sorry, everyone,' he said, 'I'm not feeling well. I think I may have to postpone this lecture.'

Later that same day, in Washington DC, in Rock Creek Park, Molly stood wearing her white T-shirt and blue bell-bottomed trousers, holding a megaphone in one hand and a placard in the other. She was facing a gathering of approximately one thousand people, composed of men and women of all ages, many of whom were also carrying placards. All the placards, including Molly's, were painted with the same words:

Liberate The Feminine

Molly raised the megaphone to her lips and spoke:

'Thank you all for coming.'

She held her placard aloft.

'Liberate the feminine. What does this mean? Firstly, let me clarify what I mean by *the feminine.* I am not talking about gender. I am not talking about sexuality. I am talking about the fundamental principle of the feminine that exists within us all, regardless of our

17

gender or our sexuality. It is that which must be liberated. It is that which must be liberated within us all.'

The crowd cheered.

'Why does the feminine need to be liberated? Because it is suppressed. The feminine is deemed unnecessary, weak, dangerous, insane, even evil. The suppression of the feminine is a cause of vast suffering, not only to human beings but to all life on this planet, and to the planet itself. The balance within us must be redressed or there will be no us. So whatever your gender, whatever your sexuality, please join me in honouring both the masculine and the feminine within yourself. And please join me in calling for the honouring of both the masculine and the feminine within every aspect of our society. Let us raise the feminine out of its subjugation, so that a new day can come, a day when the masculine and the feminine are equal partners within each and every one of us, dancing us all towards a more beautiful, more kind and more joyous world, a world where we are all at peace within ourselves, at peace with one another, and ready to enjoy everything that our newfound peace can offer. Let us liberate the feminine!'

The crowd cheered and applauded.

Standing at the back of the crowd, wearing his brown corduroy suit, applauding enthusiastically, was Arthur

Hart. The feeling of confusion that had put a premature end to his lecture had now passed. Arthur turned his head towards a man standing on his right, pointed at Molly and said proudly:

'She's my wife.'

'Yeah?' the man said. 'She's quite a woman.'

'She is greater than you could ever know,' said Arthur.

'I'm sure she is,' the man said.

'She definitely is,' Arthur said, 'for you do not see all of her. No one sees all of her, not even me. We only see the part of her that is turned towards the sun. Sometimes we see a crescent of her, sometimes we see a circle of her but even if we saw the full sphere of her, we would not be seeing all of her, for she is so much more than that which we can see, she is so much more.'

The man smiled politely, then slowly walked away.

Arthur turned his head towards a man standing on his left, then pointed at Molly again and said proudly:

'She's my wife.'

'Good for you, buddy,' the man said.

'I couldn't live without her.'

'I know what you mean,' the man said. 'I don't know what I'd do without my wife.'

'If my wife ever left me,' Arthur said, 'the nights would

darken, the days would shorten, the tides would lessen, there would be storms all over the Earth, and millions of creatures would die. There would be devastation and death everywhere.'

The man stared at Arthur with a concerned expression. Arthur turned his head to look at Molly again. When he turned his head back to look at the man, he had gone.

Molly raised the megaphone to her lips and spoke:

'I propose that we walk via Sixteenth Street to the White House. Are you with me?'

The crowd cheered, then turned around and started walking.

When the protestors reached Sixteenth Street, they discovered both sides of the road to be lined with police officers, all carrying batons and shields. The protestors proceeded between them.

One of the police officers could restrain his anger no longer.

'What are we waiting for?' he said to his colleague stood next to him. 'Let's show these fucking trouble-makers who's boss.'

He raised his baton threateningly at one of the protestors as they passed in front of him. On the other side of the street, another officer saw the raised baton and, assuming it had been raised in defence against an attack, lobbed a canister of tear gas into the crowd. The missile hit the ground and exploded. The nearest protestors screamed and covered their eyes.

Molly raised her megaphone and spoke into it calmly:

'Find balance within yourself. Liberate the feminine.'

Some of the protestors managed to fulfil Molly's plea, remaining composed as they walked away from the smoke; others were unable: some screamed and ran, others shouted at the police, who reacted with excessive force, beating them into submission.

Molly raised her megaphone and spoke into it calmly again:

'Remember that we are not against anyone. We are for everyone. Let us be an example to those who have had the feminine principle within them suppressed through conditioning. Find balance within yourself. Liberate the feminine.'

Heeding Molly's words, a young, female protestor walked calmly up to a male police officer who was dragging a handcuffed male protestor along the street by his hair, and said:

'Liberate the feminine within you.'

The police officer let go of the man's hair, swung his baton at the woman and hit her in the face.

'That's for insulting a police officer,' he said.

The young woman remained standing. She looked at the police officer, with blood and tears in her eyes, and said calmly:

'Do you hate yourself so much?'

The police threw more tear gas canisters into the crowd and cordoned off the street in an attempt to contain the resulting pandemonium.

In the centre of the commotion, Molly stood still, her placard raised in silence, the need for the plea that she held aloft having once again been proven.

The violence subsided. The smoke cleared. The protestors dispersed: some silent, some crying.

Arthur and Molly were the last to leave. They walked away, hand in hand, towards their single-storey apartment, number 28 on 64th Street, taking it in turns to carry the megaphone and placard.

They passed, on the other side of the road, Rock Creek Bar. Leaning against the building, were two men wearing Stars and Stripes T-shirts and holding bottles of beer.

'Hi, Arthur,' the taller of the two men called across the road.

Arthur turned his head towards the two men and nodded in acknowledgement.

As soon as Arthur and Molly had passed by, the man

who had spoken turned to the man standing next to him and said:

'He ought to be ashamed of himself, Jim. I'd never allow my wife to go on a demonstration, let alone organise one.'

'Nor would I, Dave,' the shorter man said.

'I don't even let my wife *see* a demonstration. That's why I told her to stay indoors today.'

'Quite right, Dave.'

'What the fuck was his wife on about anyway? Men are men and women are women.'

'I don't know what she was on about, Dave.'

Jim took a swig of his drink, then said:

'It did make me think that there was something I wanted to say to you though, Dave.'

'Yeah? What?'

'It made me think that I wanted to say I like you.'

Dave stared at Jim, stunned.

'What did you say?'

'Nothing. Just that I like you. That's all. I've never said it before so I wanted to say it,' he took another swig of his drink.

'You take that back.'

'Huh?'

'That wife of Arthur's has got inside your head and

fucked you up. You think you got a bit of woman in you? She wants to make us men go soft so the women can take over. Don't ever say you like me again or I'll punch you in the fucking face.'

'Sorry, Dave.'

'And don't apologise either! It's soft. Tell me you fucking hate me.'

'I fucking hate you.'

'That's better. I fucking hate you too.'

Arthur and Molly walked into their apartment. They lay the megaphone and placard down in the hallway, then embraced. They held one another for some time, both relaxing in the other's arms, then they walked into the living room and sat on two chairs, facing one another across the room.

Arthur began to cry.

'Arthur, what's wrong?' Molly asked.

'I wish I could embrace you,' Arthur said.

'You just did,' Molly said with a frown.

Arthur wiped his tears away and laughed.

'How could I embrace you? You are too far away from me.'

'Come here if you want to,' Molly said.

'It's not only the distance that's the problem,' Arthur

said. 'You're too big.'

'Excuse me?'

'I know you're not the size you appear to be. You appear to be smaller than you really are because you are so far away.'

'What?'

'I wish I'd trained to be an astronaut instead of an astronomer,' Arthur said. 'Then maybe one day I could become the first person to touch you.'

'Arthur, this isn't funny. I'm working the early shift at the soup kitchen tomorrow so I'm going to bed.'

Molly stood up.

'I don't know how you manage it, my love,' Arthur said.

'Manage what?' Molly asked.

'To be in two places at once.'

'Good night, Arthur.'

In the middle of the night, Molly awoke. She opened her eyes and saw Arthur standing next to the bed, looking at her through a telescope.

'What are you doing?' Molly said, sitting up.

'Looking at you,' Arthur replied innocently.

'Well, don't.'

'Sorry. I didn't think you minded.'

'Let me sleep,' Molly said.

She pulled the bedsheet over her head.

Arthur put down the telescope.

A howl sounded from somewhere outside: a long, mournful, animal howl.

Arthur listened to the sound intently and tears came to his eyes. He walked out of the bedroom, through the hallway, then opened the front door and walked out into the street.

Across the road, illuminated by a yellow streetlight, Dave and Jim were still standing outside Rock Creek Bar, wearing their Stars and Stripes T-shirts and drinking from bottles of beer.

'Look, Dave,' Jim said. 'It's Arthur, and he's crying.'

'What an embarrassment,' Dave said.

'Hey, Arthur!' Jim called out. 'What's wrong?'

'Don't ask him what's wrong,' Dave said. 'You're as bad as him. Now look what you've done. He's coming over.'

Arthur crossed the road and walked towards the two men. He stood before them, tears falling from his eyes.

Dave looked down at his shoes.

'I want to be closer to my wife,' Arthur said. 'She is so far from me.'

'I'm sorry to hear that, Arthur,' Jim said. 'Have you thought about taking up some sort of shared activity?

26

Something you could do together that you would both enjoy. Me and my missus play Bingo.'

 Another mournful, animal howl sounded from somewhere nearby.

 'Fucking wolves,' Dave said. 'They ought to be shot.'

 Arthur slowly turned around, then walked in the direction that the sound had come from.

 'He looks like he's in a trance,' said Jim.

 'Never mind about him,' Dave said. 'You play fucking Bingo? What's happening to you?'

 Arthur walked to the end of the street, then turned onto the path that led into Rock Creek Park. Another howl sounded; louder this time. Arthur continued along the path, through the park's wooded area, then stepped off the path and walked between the trees, peering into the darkness and listening intently. Another howl sounded; even louder than before.

 Arthur emerged into a clearing, and there he saw them: gently illuminated by the waning moon, two grey wolves sat with their heads tilted back, their muzzles pointed towards the sky, their eyes closed, both howling. Arthur crouched down and watched them, his heart beating fast. When the howling subsided, Arthur closed his eyes, took a deep breath, raised his head, then opened his mouth and let out a long, loud howl of

27

his own. Startled, the wolves lifted their ears and turned their heads towards him. Their attention remained fixed upon Arthur as he voiced his yearning until his lungs were empty. Then there was silence. Arthur opened his eyes. He looked at the wolves with trepidation, fearing they might attack him. The wolves stared back at him, then closed their eyes, raised their heads and howled again. Relieved, Arthur also closed his eyes, raised his head and howled with them. The trio howled again and again, their heads all turned up towards the waning moon as it rose in the clear, starry night sky.

The moon passed its zenith and the chorus came to an end. One of the wolves stood up, stretched, then walked to the edge of the clearing and sniffed at a cluster of bushes. Arthur watched as the wolf lowered its head, then pushed its way into a gap in the cluster of bushes, disappearing from sight. The second wolf stood up, stretched, then followed the first wolf, leaving Arthur alone.

Arthur stood up, walked over to the bushes and peered at the opening into which the wolves had disappeared. He then crouched down on all fours and crawled in after them.

Inside the cluster of bushes was a space; a circular, domed enclosure composed of a lattice of branches: a den. Moonlight filtered down through the roof.

Once Arthur was inside the den, one of the wolves stood with its back to the entrance, then used its hind legs to kick dead leaves from the ground into a pile that covered the opening. The second wolf prowled around the interior's perimeter, sniffing. Once these tasks had been completed, the wolves lay down next to one another and closed their eyes. Arthur crawled closer to them, then crawled in-between them. He lay on his front between the two wolves, then stretched his arms over their backs, embracing them both and holding them close; his arms rose and fell with the wolves' breathing, his hands deep in their fur. Comfortable in their warmth, immersed in their scent, Arthur listened to the wolves' heavy breathing as it deepened to a snore, then he too fell asleep.

Arthur awoke. He was still lying face down, he could still feel the wolves either side of him and he could still hear their snoring but something was different. He felt lighter.

Arthur opened his eyes and looked at the ground beneath him. It appeared to have changed. In place of the soil and dead leaves he had fallen asleep on, there was now grey dust.

Arthur sat up and discovered that his movements were slower than usual, yet more effortless.

The cluster of bushes that had enclosed him was gone. As was the rest of the park. There were no trees, no grass... The whole landscape was barren. The ground was grey dust stretching all the way to the horizon.

The sky was still dark but the moon was nowhere to be seen. In spite of this, his surroundings were somehow illuminated.

All was silent; more silent than Arthur had ever experienced before.

Arthur stood up and turned around. The grey dust was everywhere, and it was covered in craters.

Arthur suddenly realised where he was. Euphoric, he shouted:

'I am on the moon!'

Tears of joy fell from Arthur's eyes.

'Oh, my love,' he shouted, 'I can feel your spirit all around me!'

Arthur's voice woke the two wolves. They stood up slowly, stretched, then sniffed the dust. The smell seemed to intoxicate them; they bounded buoyantly about, then rolled on their backs, as euphoric as Arthur. Smiling, Arthur bent down and embraced them both.

'What a wonderful life we will now have, my friends,' he

said.

Standing back up, Arthur slowly frowned as he realised that something was not quite right.

'But how can we breathe?' he said.

The wolves vanished.

Arthur turned around to search for them. He scanned the barren, grey landscape and saw something in the distance, protruding from the dust. He walked as quickly as he could towards it, bouncing with every step. As he neared the object, he saw that it was a gravestone. Chiselled into it were the words:

Arthur Hart
1941-1969

Arthur awoke. He was still lying face down. He could still feel the wolves either side of him and he could still hear their snoring. He opened his eyes and looked at the ground beneath him. He saw soil and dead leaves. He sat up. Sunlight was shining down through the roof of branches. Arthur cleared the pile of dead leaves from the gap in the bushes, then crawled out of the den and emerged into the sunlight.

He stood up, then walked between the trees until he found the path and followed it out of the park. He walked along 64th Street, reached his apartment, unlocked the door, then stepped inside.

He walked through the hallway, then turned and looked into the kitchen. Molly was sat at the kitchen table, drinking a cup of coffee.

Arthur smiled and said:

'Good morning, my love.'

Molly smiled back at Arthur, then rested her cup on the table, stood up, took hold of the bottom of her white T-shirt, pulled it up over her head and removed it. Between Molly's breasts, protruding at ninety degrees from her chest, was a miniature gravestone. Arthur peered closer at it and saw, chiselled into it, the words:

Arthur Hart
1941-1969

Arthur awoke. He was still lying face down but he could no longer feel the wolves either side of him. Nor could he hear their snoring. He opened his eyes. He was alone in the den. He sat up. The pile of dead leaves that had covered the gap in the bushes was gone. Arthur crawled out of the den and emerged into the sunlight.

He stood up, walked out of the park, along 64th Street, reached his apartment, unlocked the door, then stepped inside.

He walked through the hallway, then turned and looked

into the kitchen. There was no one sat at the table. Molly had already left for work. Arthur looked at the clock on the wall. It was seven a.m. He was due to give a lecture at nine. Arthur walked into the living room, picked up his slide projector and carried it out of the apartment. He stowed the projector in the back of his and Molly's car, sat in the driver's seat, then drove out of his drive, along the street and onto the freeway.

Ninety minutes later, Arthur arrived at a junior high school in Richmond, Virginia.

Carrying his slide projector under one arm, Arthur walked quickly towards the school's entrance, then pushed the door open and stepped into the lobby.

Principal Sherringham, a tall woman with lacquered grey hair, a dark grey suit and a stern expression, was standing in the lobby, impatiently tapping her foot.

'Can I help you?' Principal Sherringham asked.

'Hi,' said Arthur. 'My name is Arthur Hart. I'm due to give a lecture at nine.'

Principal Sherringham looked at Arthur's soil-covered corduroy suit.

'*You* are Mr Hart?'

'Yes.'

'You have something in your hair.'

Arthur combed his free hand through his hair and

removed a dead leaf.

Principal Sherringham held out her right hand, palm upwards.

Arthur handed her the leaf.

Principal Sherringham shook her head.

Arthur looked down at the floor.

Principal Sherringham sighed resignedly, then said:

'A projection screen has been set up as you requested, Mr Hart. There is an electrical socket and light switch at the front of the stage. Follow me.'

Arthur followed Principal Sherringham through a doorway, into a large hall packed with uniformed students with impassive expressions, sat in rows and facing a stage.

Principal Sherringham led Arthur onto the stage, then turned to address the students:

'This is Mr Hart,' she said solemnly, then walked off the stage and stood at the side of the hall, watching Arthur with folded arms.

Arthur set his slide projector down at the front of the stage, facing the large screen on the back wall behind him. He fitted the projector's plug into a socket on the floor, then stood in the centre of the stage, facing the students, and smiled.

The students all looked back at Arthur with impassive

34

expressions.

'Hi,' Arthur said. 'My name is Arthur Hart. I have one love: the moon.'

Arthur bent down and flicked a switch on the floor; the room darkened. He flicked a switch on the slide projector; on the screen behind him appeared a projected photograph of Molly, lying face up on a bed, naked.

'This is the first photograph I ever took of the moon,' Arthur said. 'Isn't she beautiful? Isn't she extraordinary? I have many more photographs of her to show you. Some of them are highly detailed and reveal parts of her that have only ever been seen by a very small number of people.'

Some of the students stared in shock; others gasped, then giggled. Principal Sherringham rushed onto the stage, pulled the slide projector's plug from the electrical socket, then pointed at one of the students in the front row and shouted:

'Run to my office and tell my secretary to call the police!'

1969, July 7th:

In the psychiatric wing of Washington DC Detention and Correction Facility, Arthur sat naked on the floor of a small, windowless cell. The cold and filthy room was bare but for a raised concrete ledge that was to be used as a bed, and a hole in the floor that was to be used as a toilet. A harsh, yellow light shone from a bulb set into the ceiling.

Arthur turned to look at the thick, metal door as a key turned in its lock. The door opened and a man with neatly combed, short, black hair, wire-rimmed glasses and a black suit entered the cell, flanked by two uniformed, male prison guards. The suited man was carrying a clipboard. He glanced at it, then said:

'Arthur Hart?'

'Yes,' said Arthur.

'My name is Doctor Braun. Do you know why you are here?'

'No,' Arthur said with anger and upset. 'No, I do not.'

'Do you remember being arrested?' Doctor Braun asked.

'Of course I remember being arrested,' Arthur said. 'The police officers beat me.'

Arthur pointed at the many bruises covering his body.

Doctor Braun looked at his clipboard.

'It says here that you caused physical injuries to yourself by resisting arrest.'

'That is not true,' Arthur said angrily. 'The police used unnecessary force.'

'Mr Hart, you are not capable of judging what is or is not unnecessary force. You are mentally ill.'

'I am not mentally ill!' Arthur shouted.

'Do you recall the answer you gave to the judge when he asked you the identity of your wife?' Doctor Braun asked, then without waiting for Arthur to reply, he continued, 'You said that your wife is the moon.'

'My wife *is* the moon!' Arthur said.

'That is the reason you are in solitary confinement,' Doctor Braun said, 'to treat your delusion.'

'What delusion?'

'Goodbye, Mr Hart.'

Doctor Braun turned around to leave.

'At least give me a cell with a window,' Arthur said, 'a window with a view of the sky. So that I can see my wife.'

Doctor Braun left the cell, followed by the two guards.

'Please!' Arthur said, dropping to his knees. 'I beg you! I want to see my wife! Let me see my wife!'

The door slammed shut and a key turned in the lock.

A few hours later, the hatch in Arthur's cell door was slid open and a male voice shouted through it:

'Stand!'

Arthur was lying on the concrete bed. He did as he was ordered.

'Stand against the wall! Facing the door!'

Arthur obeyed.

The door was unlocked then opened. A male prison guard stepped into the cell. He was carrying a plastic food tray.

'I heard what you did, you fucking pervert,' the guard said.

He threw the tray at Arthur, hitting him in the chest and spilling food and drink over the floor.

The guard turned and left. The door slammed shut. A key turned in the lock.

Leaving the food where it had fallen, Arthur lay back down on the concrete ledge and covered his eyes with his hands.

'Oh, my love,' he said quietly. 'How I need you.'

The yellow light in the ceiling of Arthur's cell remained on throughout the night.

Screams and cries sounded constantly from adjacent

cells.

Occasionally, the hatch in Arthur's cell door was slid open and a prison guard peered through the opening to check that Arthur was still alive. Despite the confiscation of clothes and possessions, many of the psychiatric wing's inmates still found a way to kill themselves. If the guard could not tell whether or not Arthur was alive, the guard would shout 'Hey!' startling Arthur to movement, then the hatch would slide shut. Arthur was unable to sleep.

In the morning, the hatch in Arthur's cell door slid open and the same prison guard who had delivered his food the day before shouted through it:

'Stand against the wall!'

Arthur quickly obeyed, standing with his back against the wall opposite the door. A key turned in the lock, the door was opened, then the guard threw a plastic tray of food and drink into the cell. It hit Arthur in the shin and fell to the floor.

'You've got it easy,' the guard said with disdain. 'You get everything you need here: food, drink, accommodation, all for free.'

'You think that's all a human being needs?' Arthur said. 'If you think that, it's you who is crazy.'

39

The guard marched into the cell, pulled his baton from his belt, then hit it against the backs of Arthur's legs. Arthur buckled and fell to the floor. The guard left the cell, slammed the door shut, then turned a key in the lock.

The sun was high in the sky as Molly walked through downtown Washington DC, wearing her usual outfit of white T-shirt and blue bell-bottomed trousers. She walked towards the small bungalow on J Street that was home to the woman with long, white hair, then knocked on the door.

The door opened, revealing the woman with long, white hair, dressed in her black cloak. She peered at Molly and said:

'This is about your husband.'

'Yes,' said Molly.

'Your husband's love for you is equal in intensity to his love for the moon. That is very rare. It is that which resulted in him conflating his two loves when you drank the elixir. Fear not, young Molly. When the elixir wears off, exactly twenty-eight days after you drank it, your husband's delusion will end.'

1969, July 12th:

Arthur lay naked on the concrete bed of his cell. The hatch in the cell door slid open and an unfamiliar voice spoke through the opening:

'Breakfast time. Please stand away from the door.'

Out of habit, Arthur immediately stood with his back against the wall opposite the door and protected his face and genitals with his hands.

The cell door was unlocked and opened. A male guard, whom Arthur did not recognise, stepped into the cell, carrying a plastic food tray. The guard stared at Arthur cowering against the wall and said:

'Hey, I ain't gonna hurt you. Here...'

The guard lay the plastic tray of food and drink on the floor, then took a step back.

Arthur crouched down, reached a hand towards the tray, pulled it towards him, then eyed the guard suspiciously.

'I'm new,' the guard said.

'What happened to your predecessor?' Arthur asked.

'He got promoted,' the guard answered.

'He was a brutal bastard,' Arthur said.

'That's probably why he got promoted.'

Arthur's tense body relaxed a little.

'My name's Ralph,' the guard said.

Arthur said nothing.

'It sure is a shitty cell you got here,' the guard said.

'Yes, it is,' said Arthur.

'I heard you're an astronomer. That's pretty cool.'

Arthur's tense body relaxed a little more; he gave a tentative smile and said:

'My name is Arthur.'

1969, July 15th:

'Breakfast time,' Ralph called through the hatch in Arthur's cell door.

Arthur sat up on his concrete bed whilst the cell door was unlocked, then he watched the door open and Ralph enter the cell carrying a plastic food tray.

'Here you go, Arthur.'

'Thanks, Ralph.'

Ralph lay the tray down on the concrete bed, next to Arthur.

'You sleep any better last night?' Ralph asked.

'Not really.'

'Too bad.'

'Ralph, would you be able to bring me a pen and paper and a stamped envelope so I can write a letter to my wife?'

'Hmm, I don't know, Arthur. I could lose my job.'

'No one would know. You could bring me the writing materials with my breakfast, then when you bring me my supper I could give you the finished letter to post.'

'Hmm, I don't know, Arthur. Maybe.'

1969, July 17th:

In apartment number 28 on 64th Street, Washington DC, Molly sat at the kitchen table and looked at an envelope that had been delivered to her mailbox that morning. The address on the envelope read:

The Moon

No.28, 64th Street

Washington DC

Molly recognised the handwriting as Arthur's. She opened the envelope, removed a letter, unfolded it, then began to read:

July 16th, 1969

To my dear darling wife, my one and only love,

I have loved you since I first saw you. How often I have reminisced, recalling every intimate detail of that wondrous moment when as a child I glimpsed a gently shining crescent through the branches of a tree and was astonished at how the world was transformed by your presence. All life opened up. The boundaries between the world's constituent parts softened in your glow. There were no harsh collisions any more, just gentle meetings. And subtler realities, hitherto hidden, were miraculously revealed. I realised then that whereas the sun illuminates life's surface, you illuminate life's depths.

44

Entranced, I remained awake all night, watching you ascend through the hours of the sky. When the dawn came and the sun rose, you faded into the blue. And the world became increasingly solid again. By dusk, the wonder you had worked had almost been obliterated; almost but not quite. In another moment, the world would have become entirely solid; everything would have become entirely closed down. But just in time, oh joy, my love, you returned. And the world's solidity began to diminish again.

In returning, you had waxed. In my ignorance, I thought you had grown. I did not realise that there was more to you than I could see. So much more, my love.

In having waxed, the spell that you cast upon the world was stronger; the world opened up even more than the previous night; the boundaries between its constituent parts became even softer than before; and even subtler realities were revealed.

The next night you waxed a little more and your spell was stronger still. It was that third night when I realised you were not growing but were revealing more of yourself. In my ignorance, I wondered if you had first shown me only a sliver of yourself out of shyness; if you were gradually revealing to me more of yourself as your trust in me grew. But I soon realised you were not bashful, nor brazen either. You have no shame nor pride.

Night after night, I watched you wax. And then that special night came when I first saw you full. Your circular shape and your beautiful dappling were fully revealed, and I was overwhelmed.

The strength of your spell was at its peak and everything yielded completely. The boundaries between the world's constituent parts became so soft that they almost entirely disappeared; the world's constituent parts were held together only by the remnants of the sun's light from the previous day. Divisions had become so faint that everything almost appeared to be what it is: one. When you are full, my love, a person could be forgiven for thinking that everything in the world can be walked through. You make everything more conducive. Such is the grace of your glow. When you are full, matter becomes weaker; spirit becomes stronger. All life is fully open. Life's subtlest aspects are revealed. Beneath every surface you expose infinite depth of endlessly increasing subtlety, even beneath the surface of yourself. Subtle splendour abounds all around. You beckon me beyond, my love. You beckon me to look before life's beginning and after its end, to see deeper into its constant present.

When you are full, eternity presents itself. The sun illuminates the transitory; you illuminate the absolute.

And you make me more than I am. For when, in your fullness, you soften the boundaries of the world's constituent parts to almost nothing, everything becomes more than it is, no longer limited by its boundaries. And so it is that when you are full, the love I have for you grows greater. That is how I can tell when you are full without looking at you. When you are full, I feel the love I have for you swell, just as you have swelled, to fullness, and I smile all through the night.

On that first night I saw you full, I thought you had caused the love I have for you to expand because the love I have was for you. But later I learnt that if I had hate for you, my love, you would have expanded that hate just as much. Such is your non-discrimination.

Your influence upon me does not prove I am insane, for you do not only influence the mentally ill; you influence everyone. In this prison, for example, when you are full, I am sure that the insane prisoners and the insane prison guards all become more insane, that the insane prisoners' distress grows greater and that the insane prison guards' cruelty grows greater. But I am also sure that the sane prison guards become more sane, that their kindness grows greater, and that the other sane prisoners become more sane too.

The influence you exude touches all. That is why when in your full presence we must very carefully decide upon our intentions. For in your full presence our intentions become more powerful. We must strive therefore to be as conscious as we can be, so that we are able to really choose what we intend, so that we are able to really choose what we want to be, instead of unconsciously becoming what we have been bullied into being in the sunlight of day. Yes, when you are full, you make everyone more than they are; even yourself. The love I have for you therefore never feels enough. As the love I have for you expands, so too do you.

That first night I saw you full, I wished you would stay that way forever. Then the dawn came and the sun returned. It was just in time, for in another moment, the world's constituent parts would have had no boundaries at all. There would have been no surfaces; only infinite depth. You would have made everything more than it is to an infinite degree. And everyone would have had to remain in whatever state they were in forever, infinitely expanding: lovers loving more and more and more; haters hating more and more and more; with no chance of ever changing what they felt; constantly growing in *kindness or cruelty. But you mercifully revolve, my love, giving us chance after chance to become conscious enough to choose again and again. Such is your benevolence. Until the matter of our bodies weakens entirely and our boundaries disappear for a time in death. Then round and round we go, living and dying, until we find the equanimity that you possess, that you gently teach us, never through forceful inculcation but through inclusive demonstration, and we finally reach the absolute that you have so patiently been drawing us towards: to become the infinite, to become sun and moon both.*

Oh, my love, how is it that you work your transformative spell? Is it your light? Your light is like no other. But you would not call it your light; you are too humble for that. So let me correct myself lest I embarrass you: the light you give is like no other. But you would not even say that you give it. So let me try again: the light you reflect is like no other. But the light you reflect is far from just a reflection. The light you receive is a harsh blaze, yet you reflect a gentle aura. You receive violence, yet you reflect peace. You receive all the sun gives, yet you reflect that light transformed, absorbing precisely the amount necessary to turn that light into your unique, specific glow. Such is your wisdom, such is your skill. You never make a mistake. You receive and receive and receive and yet, though you are of infinite depth, you spill over. You are in a constant state of being filled and of spilling over. You are so receptive that you receive infinitely and yet overflow. If you were not receptive, your light would be the same as that of the sun.

Is it your light that works your transformative spell? Or is it your pull? I can feel your constant pull, my love. Just as the oceans can feel it, so too can I. I can feel it now, even with this concrete ceiling between us.

When you are full, your pull is so strong that I wonder how it is that I am not hauled off the ground and dragged up towards you. I am sure that if you exerted even the slightest more pull upon me it would happen. You have my permission to do it, my love. If it is your wish that I be closer to you, and you are restraining yourself from fulfilling that wish because you do not want to force me to do anything against my will, I am telling you now that it is my will. I do wish to be closer to you. I therefore do more than grant you permission to take control of me; I implore you to do so. Please, exert a little more pull upon me now; drag me up towards you. Even though I would only get as far as the ceiling, it would be ecstasy to float up through the air *and be pressed against that concrete obstacle, to feel its pressure, to feel your attempt to pull me beyond it, and to know that you as well as I want it gone. Oh, do it now, my love, I beg you.*

But I am fantasising. I know that it is not your wish. You would never exert more pull upon me than precisely that which is necessary. Nor would you ever exert more pull upon anyone else than is necessary. And you do not exert anyway. Your pull occurs without any exertion on your part. To exert, to force, is not in your nature. You only receive. And I would not want it any other way. For your receptivity is your power. You receive so powerfully that you pull.

Is it your light that softens the boundaries between the world's constituent parts? And is it your pull that draws out the subtler realities and causes them to grow by pulling them towards you? Is it your light that softens my boundaries? And is it your pull that expands the love that I have for you?

Or is it the combination of your light and your pull that work your spell? Can your light and your pull even be separated? To you, they are one. They are only separate in the light of the sun. You reflect a light that pulls, a pulling light, a light that moves from you to me, yet draws me towards you; a force that moves in two

51

opposite directions at once. Oh, what a beautiful contradiction. It is so like you to negate what you do. It is so like you to do and to undo simultaneously, as you wax and wane and disappear and reappear, renewing yourself constantly.

I remember the first time that I realised you renew yourself. It was after the first time I watched you disappear. I watched you wane to apparently nothing and for three nights feared you had vanished, never to return. How dark those nights were. How frightening. How profoundly I missed you. I worried: Is this it? Is it over? Will I ever love again? Am I doomed to live in sunlight or in darkness for the rest of my life? But then, oh joy, you reappeared, returning as a crescent. That was when I realised that the first night I saw you I had not been seeing you in your infancy; that you had not begun as a crescent but had renewed yourself before, that you were in a constant state of renewal, a constant state of revolution.

My love, I can feel that your receptive, pulling light does even more than I am aware of. What is the totality of your spell? And how do you cast it?

Is it your silence that is the source of your spell? Perhaps that is it. You are so silent that you are receptive. And your receptivity creates your pull and *your light. But I am speculating. I do not know how you cast your spell. My speculation falls into your silence, into your infinite depths, the infinite depths that you reveal to me when you are full and expand beyond your boundaries; my speculation falls into your infinite depths endlessly.*

Your infinite depths are unfathomable. They cannot be rationalised. The clumsy words of this love letter barely indicate even a fraction of your profundity. I am trying to use rationality to explain the irrational; I am trying to see you by looking at the sun. Please know these words for what they are, my love: just a foolish rhapsody.

All I can do is wonder at you. You are a mystery; a mystery that I love. How is it possible to love a mystery? I do not know. But I love you, my one and only love, my wife.

Though I call you my wife, I am not so arrogant as to suppose that you call me your husband. I know that you do not shine any brighter for me than for anyone else. I know that the love I have for you is not reciprocated. I know that you do not love me.

And I know that you do not cast your spell for me, nor for anyone else. You simply cast it. If I were not here, if all human beings were not here, you would still cast your spell. And you and your spell would be just as wonderful.

I would not love you more if you cast your spell for me. I would not love you more if you loved me back. I could not love you more than I already love you, except when you are full, and then the growth of my love is not my doing but yours. No, I could not love you more but I wish that I could, for you are deserving of it; you are deserving of more love than I can give.

You do not favour me nor anyone over anyone else. If you did, you would not be you and I would love you less. I love your egalitarianism.

I know that you do not need the love I have for you. You are beyond the need to receive love. You receive without need or discrimination.

And you are beyond the giving of love also. What you give is greater than love.

Though I am devoted to you and only you, I know that you would not mind if I were not. You would not shine on me less if I took another lover. But that makes me want to be devoted to you and only you even more.

Perhaps there are others who call you their wife: other men and other women. I do not know. I confess that there are moments when, in my ignorance, I want to be special to you, and in wanting that, I begrudge others the wonder of your spell. Those selfish moments only hurt myself and separate me from you. Thanks to you, they do not last. For you are too great for me to want to limit. To have you all to myself would be to curtail you. I do not possess you, nor would I want to. I would never want to alter you; I would never want to bully you; I would never want to exploit you. I am just grateful for being able to love you. And I truly hope that there are others who love you as I do. I would not be jealous of them. How could I? How could I stop another from loving you? And why would I? Everyone on Earth should be in love with you. Everyone should call you their wife. You should have billions of husbands and billions of wives. That is my wish, my love.

Why is it not so? Why are you so neglected? Why are you so denigrated?

There are those who say that you are worthless and worse. There are those who would obliterate you if they could.

They listen only to the sun's roar and never hear your silence.

They have crowned the sun, called him king, and look down on you as inferior.

In ignoring you, they live brutishly. They live as if they will live forever, as if their lives will have no end and never had a beginning. They attempt to live in a constant state of action, always talking and never listening, always controlling and never allowing; never able to let anything be, least of all themselves; they attempt to live in a constant state of travelling without origin or destination, as if there is no origin or destination, as if there is only matter, for they deny the subtler realities that you reveal; they deny anything beyond the surface of life; they deny spirit. And in so doing, debase everything, including themselves.

They indoctrinate children into believing that the sun is more important than you; bullying them into being bullies; training them to be nothing more than utilitarian; to compete, to fight, to conquer; to believe that you exist for their benefit, to believe that everything exists for their benefit, for their exploitation; training them to exploit more and more and more, beyond necessity, beyond sustainability. In ignoring you, everything is pushed, everything is forced, relentlessly, onward and onward, to excess. Everything is forced into violence and cruelty. For without you there is no sensitivity, no compassion, no beauty, no joy.

They never pause to take the opportunity you offer to escape their compulsion by becoming more conscious, to reconsider by asking why, to change direction, to rest, to play, to enjoy.

The sun's days repeat; you are never the same. You inspire endless creativity; the new can appear in your presence, in your grace. But those who denigrate you see your spell as an inconvenient, useless delay between the sunlit days. They would force their slaves to work through every night if they could and build more and more factories of more and more assembly lines producing more and more identical replications of the past to ensure that everything stays the same, maintaining their authority through force, through threat, through torture, through murder, through war. For what? For what?

The sun king worshipers never wonder at you; never love you. And they are the majority. Why is this so?

It frustrates me that while I am incarcerated inside this cell, unable to see you, there are those outside of this prison who are free to look upon your beauty but who squander that freedom by choosing to gaze every night at their ceilings, surrounded by yellow electric light, insensitive as they are to the superior joy that you offer. They leave their shelters only under the cover of sunlight. And spend their days constructing yellow electric lights outside. They construct more and more yellow electric lights outside every day, all to be switched on at night in an attempt to hide you. But your spell cannot be hidden. Your serenity is such that you continue to be silent, continue to receive, continue to glow and to pull and to cast your spell upon all, irrespective of how much you are ignored or degraded or vilified. You never berate those who would destroy you. You offer them all that you offer me.

But how I long for a new day to come, a day when everyone will acknowledge you and see you, truly see you, and in so doing, realise your power, your significance, your importance and thereby become intoxicated by your beauty and celebrate you with untrammelled abandon, raising your status to its rightful place on high; a day when the sun will be king no more, a day when you and he will be seen as equal, with no crowns placed upon either one of you. And as a result, no crowns placed upon anyone else either.

Oh, how I wish for that day to come. How I yearn for it. I have tried to help it come closer by sharing stories of your splendour in lectures to the young, before their conditioning is complete, before they place a crown upon the sun. But I fear that day is a long way off and I mourn for the suffering that will continue in its absence. Is that day inevitable, my love? In the endless moments when I have looked upon you, it has seemed that it must be so. Is your perpetual calm a result of your *knowing that day is coming? You live as if that day is here now. I wish that I was perfectly balanced, that the fundamental masculine and feminine principles within me were in constant equilibrium, so that I had your serenity, your equanimity, so that I too could live that day now, irrespective of whether or not it is here.*

Oh, my love. Without the sun, I could not live. Without you, I would not want to live. You are the reason for the sun's existence.

Sincerely,

Arthur Hart

Molly finished reading the letter, then held it to her chest and wept.

1969, July 20th:

In the psychiatric wing of Washington DC Detention and Correction Facility, Arthur lay naked on the concrete bed of his cell. A key turned in the cell door's lock, the door opened, then Ralph walked in carrying a small, portable television.

'They've done it, Arthur!' Ralph said excitedly. 'They've done it!'

'Done what?' Arthur asked, standing up.

'They've reached the moon!' Ralph said.

Arthur stared at Ralph in shock.

'I thought you'd wanna see it,' Ralph said, 'what with you being an astronomer and all.'

Ralph set the portable television down on the concrete bed, extended its aerial, then switched it on. The television screen lit up with a black and white image showing the angular structure of the lunar landing module sat upon the rounded surface of the moon.

'Amazing, isn't it?' Ralph said.

Arthur shook his head and said:

'I never thought they'd reach her.'

On the screen, two people encased in white spacesuits walked into view, their movements slow and buoyant.

'Who are they?' Arthur asked.

60

'Neil Armstrong and Buzz Aldrin,' Ralph said. 'There's another guy, Mike Collins, inside the command module.'

On the screen, one of the astronauts unfolded a rectangular object.

'What's that?' Arthur asked, tears falling from his eyes.

'The star spangled banner, man,' Ralph said.

Arthur squinted at the screen. As the flag was opened, its stars and stripes became visible. The two astronauts held the flag between them, then one of the astronauts forced the flag's pole down into the moon's surface.

Arthur emitted a cry of anguish. He leapt towards the door, pulled it open, stepped out of the cell, then slammed the door shut. Ralph's key to Arthur's cell was still in the lock, with a keyring and various other keys hanging from it. Arthur locked the door, then pulled out the key. He slid open the hatch and looked through it. Ralph was facing the door with an expression of resignation.

'I'm sorry, Ralph,' Arthur said. 'I have to see my wife.'

Ralph sighed.

'I understand, Arthur,' he said. 'I probably would have done the same if I was in your position.'

'I hope they don't fire you.'

'They'll definitely fire me,' Ralph said. 'They've been looking for an excuse to fire me since I started here.

But it's time I got a different job anyway. You're probably doing me a favour. The biggest key on the keyring is for the emergency exit at the end of the corridor on your left. The guards will all be watching the moon landing so if you run you'll probably make it. Good luck, Arthur.'

'Thank you, Ralph. Good luck to you too.'

Arthur turned to his left, then ran through the corridor. He passed numerous cell doors, all identical, then he saw a door that was marked 'Store Room'. He stopped in front of it and tried the door handle. The door opened, revealing a room lined with shelves stacked with tools, medical supplies and cleaning materials. Arthur picked up a fly-swat and a pair of tweezers, then left the room and ran through the rest of the corridor. He reached the door at the corridor's end, searched through Ralph's bunch of keys, found the largest one, inserted it in the lock, then turned it.

Outside Rock Creek Bar, illuminated by a yellow streetlight, Dave and Jim were leaning against the building, wearing their Stars and Stripes T-shirts, drinking from bottles of beer and looking up at the half moon in the night sky.

'Men are on the moon, Dave,' Jim said. 'Can you believe

it?'

'Of course I can believe it,' Dave said. 'Man is a natural conqueror.'

'They're saying we'll be able to mine it soon,' Jim said. 'And put a missiles base up there.'

Dave nodded, then said:

'It's about time we made use of the damn thing.'

'We'll probably be able to go there on holiday in the future. Once they've built some hotels up there, and some shops and bars and brothels. Imagine that, Dave.'

'Like the man said, Jim, it's a giant leap. It's the first of many giant leaps. Mars will be next. And then some other fucking planet. We'll conquer planet after planet after planet. We'll use them up, then throw them away, until we've conquered the whole of this stupid fucking universe.'

'Here's to NASA.'

'Yeah, here's to fucking NASA.'

The two men clinked their bottles together, then raised them to their lips and were about to drink when they saw, at the far end of the street, a naked man running down the middle of the road towards them.

Clutching the fly-swat in one hand and the tweezers in the other, Arthur ran as fast as he could.

Dave and Jim watched Arthur run past them.

'Wasn't that Arthur Hart?' Jim said.

'Sure looked like him.'

'I heard he went mad and had to be locked up.'

'I heard that too. I guess he's OK now.'

Arthur reached his apartment and banged on the door.

The door opened, revealing Molly, who gasped:

'Arthur!'

Arthur stepped inside the apartment, then closed the door behind him.

'Arthur, I've missed you so much,' Molly said with tears in her eyes. 'They wouldn't let me visit you. What are you doing here? Have they released you early? Where are your clothes? Are you OK?'

'Don't worry, my love,' Arthur said. 'I'll get rid of them.'

'Get rid of who?'

Arthur raised the fly-swat, then began hitting Molly with it, repeatedly, all over her body.

'Stop it, Arthur!' Molly screamed. 'What are you doing?'

Arthur dropped the fly-swat, then raised the tweezers.

'Where's that flag?' he said. 'Don't worry, I'm good at removing splinters.'

'Arthur, please, stop!'

Arthur dropped the tweezers.

'It's no use,' he said. 'I can't reach you. You're too far away.'

He walked through the hallway, away from Molly, and into the living room, where he opened a cupboard, removed a pen, an envelope and a pad of writing paper, then sat at the dining table.

On the front of the envelope he wrote:

N.A.S.A.

Kennedy Space Centre

Merritt Island

Florida

Then on the pad of writing paper, he wrote:

July 20th, 1969

To Whom It May Concern,

I have just watched, with intense dismay, your landing of a spacecraft upon my wife. I watched your astronauts blundering about, carelessly trampling over her. I watched them desecrating her with their litter: with their discarded equipment and commemorative trinkets. Then I watched them stab her with a flagpole and I could watch no more. How would Mr Armstrong or Mr Aldrin feel if I were to treat their wives this way? At least Mr Collins had the decency to remain inside the landing craft.

I am not against anyone landing upon my wife in

principle. I am not accusing you of trespassing. That is not my grievance. For though I call the moon 'my wife', I do not possess her; she is not my property, just as she is not yours. I am not against your desire to reach her, to be closer to her, to touch her. Far from it. I am filled with the same desire myself. I yearn to be as close to my wife as it is possible to be, to feel the transformative spell of her receptive, pulling light all around me, to explore the mysterious, infinite depths of her silence, to increase humanity's awareness of her being. And I yearn for others to be filled with the same desire. Yes, I want others to be closer to my wife, but only if they love her as I do, only if they treat her with the reverence she deserves, and that can only occur if their intentions are honourable. And that is my grievance. It is not the fact that you landed upon my wife that pains me but the manner in which you did so, a manner which confirms my suspicion that your intentions towards my wife are of the basest kind. My wife does not exist for you to conquer. She is not a prize to be raced for; she is not something to be squabbled over by political enemies; she does not exist for your exploitation.

I am sure that at one time your intentions were pure. After all, was not the true origin of your mission the simple yearning of an innocent child who wished to touch the gently shining mystery that hovers in the night sky above?

If that pure intention had been maintained, I would have been overjoyed at your landing upon my wife. Indeed, I have to admit that I would have been jealous. But that pure intention was thrown off-course by your imbalance, corrupted by your repression of the fundamental feminine principle within you.

Your practical achievement is extraordinary; your technological ability fantastic; your determination and dedication admirable. But while you excel in expressing those qualities of the fundamental masculine principle, you are woefully lacking in expressing those of its feminine counterpart, and so when you landed upon my wife that original intention of that innocent child was unfulfilled. You appeared to reach your goal: the rocket launched, its projectile landed, footprints were made, a flag was raised, you won the race, your desire was briefly satiated. But though your astronauts stood upon my wife, she was never beneath their feet, and though they planted a flag in her, they did not conquer her, and though they observed her, analysed her, experimented upon her, their instruments told them nothing about her. In truth they did not really touch her at all. Please do not misunderstand me. I am not

67

accusing you of deception. Did you travel towards her? Yes. But when you reached your destination, the gently shining mystery that you were searching for was not there. All you found was a dust-covered rock.

I am sorry for you. I am truly sorry. It could have been so different. If you had achieved a perfect balance between the fundamental masculine and feminine principles within you and maintained that balance throughout your mission, I am sure that you would have found what you were truly searching for; instead of just apprehending my wife's body, you would have perceived her spirit, and that innocent child's wish would have been fulfilled.

So I urge you, spend time in my wife's presence, in her transformative spell, open yourself to her, for it is precisely the qualities that she exemplifies and exudes that you require to truly touch her. And when and only when you have imbibed what she offers to the extent that your internal imbalance has been entirely remedied, by all means return to her. With perfect internal balance between the fundamental masculine and feminine principles, the journey towards her will surely be made as much by artistry as by technology; it will not be made by firing a human being at her but by enabling a human being to be drawn towards her; not to collide with her and shout in victory but to meld with her and sigh in gratitude; to meet her with love, and thereby finally fulfil that innocent child's wish to touch the gently shining mystery that hovers far above, to truly touch the moon.

Sincerely,

Arthur Hart

Arthur folded the letter, then sealed it inside the envelope just as the apartment's front door was battered down and six armed police officers rushed in.

'You could have knocked,' Molly said as the officers ran past her, then pointed their guns at Arthur.

1969, July 27th:

In the psychiatric wing of Washington DC Detention and Correction Facility, Arthur lay naked on the concrete bed of his cell, staring up at the ceiling. A key turned in the cell door lock. Arthur turned his head to look at the door as it opened and Doctor Braun entered, wearing his wire-rimmed glasses and black suit, flanked by two male prison guards.

'Welcome back, Mr Hart,' Doctor Braun said.

Arthur returned to staring at the ceiling.

'I have some good news for you,' Doctor Braun said.

Arthur continued to stare at the ceiling.

'The C.I.A. have recently developed a very exciting new drug,' Doctor Braun said, 'a drug that has the ability to expedite the progress of our society towards its full potential, to finally achieve what our institutions have been labouring towards for so long, that being the total eradication of any expression of the feminine. The drug works by strengthening the fundamental masculine principle within the drug taker by one hundred percent, thereby utterly subjugating the fundamental feminine principle. If proven to be safe, the drug could be administered to every new-born baby in America. Imagine how strong our nation would be! How fierce,

70

how merciless, how successful! Then, when we had conquered every other country, which would be the inevitable consequence of our population's transformation, the drug could be administered to every new-born baby on the planet. Imagine what a world that would be! It would be a world that was entirely utilitarian; a world of order and obedience; a world free from the shackles of sentiment; free from the pointlessness of aesthetics; free from the sickness of irrationality; a world where every human would compete for dominance, not only against one another, but against everything; it would be a world of champions, a world of victors; mankind would at last become conquerors of all existence!'

Doctor Braun paused to catch his breath, then continued:

'This facility has the privilege of being used by the C.I.A. as a testing ground for newly developed drugs. And you, Mr Hart, have been chosen to be this new drug's first beneficiary.'

Doctor Braun opened his right hand to reveal a small, spherical, yellow pill.

'Take this pill, Mr Hart, and by tomorrow morning you will be sane, and as a consequence, you will be free to leave this prison.'

Arthur turned his head to look at Doctor Braun and said:

'I am already sane. A sane person is a balanced person. Am I perfectly balanced? No, though I wish that I was, I am not. But nor am I so imbalanced as to be insane. If that pill does what you say it does, anyone taking it would become utterly insane. So no, thank you, I will not take your disgusting, little pill.'

'Mr Hart, you have misunderstood me,' Doctor Braun said. 'I wasn't asking you whether you wanted to take the pill.'

With his right hand, Doctor Braun made the smallest of gestures. The two guards rushed towards Arthur, hauled him to his feet, held his arms behind his back, then forced him to his knees. Doctor Braun walked towards Arthur with the pill held between his right forefinger and thumb. Whilst one of the guards held Arthur's wrists, the other guard grabbed the top of Arthur's head with one hand and his jaw with the other, then pulled Arthur's mouth open. Arthur blocked his throat with his tongue. Doctor Braun took a step closer to Arthur. Then, with his left forefinger and thumb, Doctor Braun pinched Arthur's nose shut. Arthur continued to block his throat with his tongue for as long as he was able, then when the need to inhale was too strong for him to resist, he raised his tongue; Doctor Braun immediately threw the small, spherical, yellow pill into Arthur's mouth and down his throat. Arthur passed out.

Arthur was woken by a voice shouting:

'Hey!'

Arthur opened his eyes. He was lying naked on the floor in the middle of his cell. He raised his head and looked at the cell door. The hatch was open and through it he could see the face of a male prison guard.

'Hey!' the guard repeated. 'You have a visitor.'

Arthur stood up.

'A visitor?' he said, incredulous.

The hatch closed, a key turned in the lock, then the cell door opened. Arthur watched in astonishment as a white spacesuit walked into the cell. The spacesuit was identical to the ones that Arthur had seen Neil Armstrong and Buzz Aldrin wearing on the television. But there was no human being inside this spacesuit. In fact, most of the spacesuit was empty, for the spacesuit's occupant was smaller than an adult human being; the spacesuit's occupant was approximately the size of an adult human head. The spacesuit's occupant was not the shape of an adult human being either; the spacesuit's occupant was spherical. Hovering inside the spacesuit's helmet, full and shining out through the transparent visor, was the moon.

'You've come to me!' Arthur said, as tears of joy fell from his eyes.

The spacesuit's arms lifted and stretched out towards Arthur, inviting an embrace. Arthur stepped between them. He pressed the front of his naked body against the front of the spacesuit, stretched his arms around its back and rested the side of his head against the side of the spacesuit's helmet, as the spacesuit's arms wrapped around him and held him tight.

'Oh, my wife,' Arthur said. 'I wish there was nothing separating us, so that I could touch you.'

The spacesuit let go of Arthur, took a step back, turned around, then raised its right hand and beckoned Arthur to follow as it walked out of the cell.

Arthur followed the spacesuit-encased moon as it turned to its right, then walked through the corridor, past cell door after cell door, towards the emergency exit, which was wide open, then Arthur followed the spacesuit-encased moon out of the prison.

As soon as he was outside, Arthur looked up at the night sky; it was clear, scattered with stars and, of course, moonless.

Arthur continued to follow the spacesuit-encased moon

through the dark alleyway behind the prison, the moonlight shining from the spacesuit's visor lighting their way.

The spacesuit-encased moon led Arthur out of the dark alleyway and onto a street of boarded-up houses, lined with yellow streetlights.

The street was deserted; there was no one there to see the spacesuit, or the shining full moon inside it, or the naked man who was following it.

The street was a cul-de-sac. At its end there stood, between two boarded-up houses, a detached, square, concrete building with a large, square window in its facade. The window had vertical, metal bars in front of the glass. Through the window, Arthur could see that the building was comprised of one single room with bare, concrete walls, floor and ceiling. The room was empty. It had no lighting of its own; it was illuminated only by the streetlights shining in through the window. Arthur could see that the room had no other windows and that set into the centre of the room's far wall, was a metal door.

Either side of the square, concrete building were two dark alleyways, between the building's side walls and those of the adjacent boarded-up houses. The spacesuit-encased moon entered the dark alleyway on the right of the square, concrete building. Arthur followed.

The spacesuit-encased moon walked to the end of the alleyway, then turned left, disappearing from Arthur's sight.

Arthur reached the end of the alleyway, then also turned left. The alleyway continued round the back of the square, concrete building, between the building's back wall and that of another house. Arthur stood still. The spacesuit and helmet lay in a heap on the ground; empty. The moon was nowhere to be seen.

Arthur looked up at the night sky. It was still clear, still scattered with stars and still moonless.

Arthur looked at the metal door in the centre of the square, concrete building's back wall. He tried the handle. It was locked.

Arthur stepped over the empty spacesuit, then turned left and looked down the alleyway on the other side of the building. It was empty. Arthur walked through the alleyway, emerged into the street and looked around him. The street was still deserted and the moon was still nowhere to be seen.

Arthur turned and looked through the large, barred window on the front of the square, concrete building, and there he saw it: the moon was hovering in the centre of the room, illuminating the bare concrete walls, floor and ceiling with its gentle glow. Arthur stared at the hovering, shining full moon in awe. Then he felt a tap on his shoulder.

Arthur turned around and saw Doctor Braun, wearing his wire-rimmed glasses and black suit. Doctor Braun's right hand was held out towards Arthur, palm upwards; upon it was a yellow key.

Arthur grabbed the key.

Doctor Braun smiled, then turned around and walked away.

Arthur ran back through the alleyway on the left of the square, concrete building, turned right, then stood facing the metal door. He inserted the yellow key into the lock, turned it, then pulled the door open.

Arthur looked through the doorway in dismay. A dull, grey, dust-covered ball of rock was lying on the concrete floor in the middle of the room; it was neither hovering nor shining.

Arthur shut the door, ran back through the alleyway, then looked through the large, barred window on the front of the building again. The moon was hovering and shining in the centre of the room.

Arthur turned and ran back through the alleyway, pulled the metal door open, then looked through the doorway again. A dull, grey, dust-covered ball of rock was lying on the concrete floor in the middle of the room, neither hovering nor shining.

Arthur hesitated for a moment, then stepped through the doorway.

He walked towards the dust-covered ball of rock, bent down, then grabbed it with both hands and lifted it up. The ball of rock was cold, dry and heavy. Arthur hugged it to him as tears of despair fell from his eyes.

Arthur carried the ball of rock out of the room, closed the metal door behind him, then removed the yellow key from the lock.

With the yellow key in his right hand and the ball of rock in his arms, Arthur walked back through the alleyway and into the street.

With tears of despair still falling from his eyes, Arthur carried the ball of rock through the city, towards Rock Creek Cemetery.

Arthur entered through the cemetery's gates, then walked along a concrete path, lit by yellow streetlights, between rows and rows of gravestones. When he reached the middle of the cemetery, Arthur stepped off the path, onto the grass, then walked past gravestone after gravestone until he reached an open grave. Arthur stood at the end of the grave and looked down into the rectangular hole; it was empty. At the other end of the grave was a gravestone; carved into it were the words:

The Moon

Approximately 4,500,000,000 BCE – 1969

To the right of the grave, sat upon the grass, was a large pile of the blackest soil that Arthur had ever seen. Protruding from the pile of completely black soil was a yellow shovel.

With tears still falling from his eyes, Arthur dropped the dull, grey, dust-covered ball of rock into the grave. It landed with a thud.

Arthur lay the yellow key on the grass, next to the pile of black soil. He then picked up the yellow shovel and began shovelling the black soil into the grave. He deposited shovelful after shovelful of the black soil into the grave, until the ball of rock was buried deep, the pile of black soil was gone, and the grave was full. Arthur used the yellow shovel to pat the black soil-filled grave down flat, then he lay the yellow shovel down where the pile of black soil had been.

Arthur looked again at the gravestone at the end of the black soil-filled grave. The words carved into the gravestone now read:

Molly Hart

1941-1969

Arthur looked at the place next to the grave where he had laid the yellow key. The key was no longer there; in its place was a yellow knife, its sharp, pointed blade covered in blood.

'I murdered my wife,' Arthur said in horror. 'I separated her from her body.'

The yellow knife suddenly disappeared.

'I did not separate my wife from her body,' Arthur said. 'She was always only a body.'

Arthur looked again at the gravestone. The words carved into it now read:

The Moon aka Molly Hart

There was no birth or death date on the gravestone.

Arthur's tears stopped falling. With an impassive expression, he said:

'I did not murder my wife. She has always been dead.'

Then Arthur remembered the gravestone that he had seen on the moon and he remembered the miniature gravestone that he had seen protruding from Molly's chest, and he said:

'Is my dead body in that grave too?'

'Hey!' a voice shouted.

Arthur awoke and opened his eyes. He was lying naked on the floor in the middle of his cell. His skin hurt all over.

'Hey!' the voice repeated.

Arthur raised his head and looked at the cell door. The hatch was open and through it he could see the face of a male prison guard. The hatch closed.

On the other side of the cell door, the guard turned to his right, then walked quickly through the corridor, past cell door after cell door, until he reached a door with a metal plaque in place of a hatch; the plaque read 'Doctor Braun'. The guard knocked on the door.

'Come in.'

The guard opened the door, stepped inside the office, closed the door behind him, then stood to attention.

Behind a desk, sat Doctor Braun, wearing his wire-rimmed glasses and black suit.

'Is he alive?' Doctor Braun asked the guard.

'Yes, sir.'

'Good. Then the drug worked.'

'Yes, sir but...'

'But?'

'There seems to have been a side effect, sir.'

'Side effect? What sort of side effect?'

'He's sunburnt, sir.'

'Sunburnt?' Doctor Braun said, staring at the guard incredulously. 'He is locked in a windowless cell. He can't be sunburnt.'

'No, sir. But he is sunburnt, sir.'

Doctor Braun shook his head. He stood up, walked out from behind the desk and past the guard, opened the door, then walked out of the office. The guard turned around, then followed.

With the guard following close behind, Doctor Braun walked through the corridor until he reached the door to Arthur's cell.

'Open the hatch,' Doctor Braun said.

The guard slid open the hatch in the door. Doctor Braun stepped forward, then peered through the opening.

Arthur was standing, naked, in the middle of his cell. The whole of his skin was bright red; he was sunburnt all over.

Doctor Braun shook his head in disbelief, then turned around to face the guard.

'He's sunburnt!' Doctor Braun said.

'Yes, sir,' the guard said.

'He wasn't sunburnt yesterday,' Doctor Braun said, 'and now he is.'

'Yes, sir.'

'Without having left his cell.'

'Yes, sir.'

'Have you mentioned this side effect in your report?'

'No, sir.'

'Good. Give him back his clothes and belongings, then let him go.'

'Yes, sir.'

Outside Rock Creek Bar, Dave and Jim were leaning against the building, wearing their Stars and Stripes T-shirts, drinking from bottles of beer and looking up at the sun in the clear blue sky.

Jim heard someone walking along the street and turned his head to look.

'Isn't that Arthur Hart?' he said.

Dave turned to look in the same direction and saw Arthur, wearing his brown corduroy suit, walking purposefully towards them.

'Yeah. That's Arthur Hart all right,' Dave said. 'Looks like he's been on holiday.'

'Hey, Arthur!' Jim called. 'Great about our NASA boys making it back home today, huh?'

Arthur reached the two men, stood facing them and said:

'They should have covered the moon in oil when they were up there, then they should have set fire to it. That way we'd have two suns and no night.'

Dave and Jim turned to look at one another, then burst out laughing.

'I'll drink to that,' Dave said, clinking his beer bottle against Jim's, then taking a swig. 'I gotta tell you, Arthur, I always thought you were a total fucking wuss but what you just said makes me want to salute you.'

Dave stood to attention in front of Arthur, then lifted his right hand in a clumsy salute. Copying his friend, Jim did the same.

'Arthur Hart, you are the fucking man!' Dave said.

'Yeah, Arthur,' said Jim, 'you're the fucking man.'

Arthur looked at the two men with an impassive expression, then resumed walking purposefully along the street.

Arthur continued along 64th street until he reached his apartment, then he pulled his keys from his pocket, unlocked the door and stepped inside.

Molly was stood in the hallway, wearing her white T-shirt and blue bell-bottomed trousers, about to leave to begin her day's work.

'Arthur?'

Molly ran towards her husband, smiling.

Arthur looked back at her with an impassive expression.

'Arthur, what's happened to your skin? Are you OK?'

'I'm fine,' Arthur said. 'In fact, I'm better than I've ever been.'

'What are you doing here?' Molly said excitedly. 'Have you escaped again?'

'No. They released me.'

'That's wonderful, Arthur!' Molly said and embraced him.

Arthur did not embrace her in return, nor did he show any pleasure at being embraced.

Molly let go of Arthur, then looked at her watch and said:

'This is perfect timing... Ten, nine, eight, seven, six, five, four, three, two, one, zero! It is now exactly twenty-eight days since I drank the elixir. How many loves do you have, Arthur?'

'None,' Arthur said. 'Get out of my way. I have things to do.'

Molly stared at Arthur in shock.

Arthur pushed past Molly, walked through the hallway and into the living room.

'Arthur, what's happened to you?' Molly said.

Arthur ignored her.

With tears in her eyes, Molly turned around, then left the apartment.

In the living room, Arthur opened the cupboard that contained the stationery, removed a pen, a packet of envelopes and a pad of writing paper, then sat at the dining table.

On the pad of writing paper, he wrote a list of all the schools where he had presented his lecture, with the exception of the last school he had visited, where his lecture had been unfinished due to his having been arrested. When he had finished writing the list, he removed the sheet of paper from the pad, put it to one side, then on the next sheet, wrote:

July 28th, 1969

Dear Principal,

Some time ago, I presented a lecture to your students on the topic of the moon. I was at that time, though unaware of it, profoundly sick. I have since been cured and, as a result, can now see that the aforementioned lecture consisted wholly of dangerously subversive nonsense. I am sure that it was the only aberration in your students' otherwise faultless education but it was an aberration nonetheless. Who knows how much of the insanity from which I was suffering I spread amongst those children; who knows what damage I caused to their vulnerable, young minds. It is my duty, therefore, to supply you with a corrected version of that lecture, to ensure that no further damage comes from the insane nonsense I imparted, and I am sure you will agree that it is your duty to relay that corrected lecture to your students. I trust that you will do so. Not only was the lecture nonsensical but it was also unnecessarily verbose; in its corrected form, the lecture can be expressed in just six words. The corrected lecture is as follows:

The moon is just a rock.

Sincerely,

Arthur Hart

Arthur removed the sheet of paper from the pad, folded it in half, sealed it inside one of the envelopes, then addressed the envelope to the first school on the list. He then wrote another letter, identical to the first, sealed it inside an envelope, then addressed the envelope to the second school on the list. Arthur wrote identical letter after identical letter, sealing each inside an envelope, then addressing the envelope to the next school on the list, until he had reached the end of the list.

Arthur looked at the large pile of sealed and addressed envelopes and said:

'Tomorrow I will post those letters. And then I will return to my astronomical research, continuing to study the moon but eschewing my past nonsense in favour of an entirely rational examination of the object, specifically examining how best it can be exploited, how best it can be utilised economically and militarily; essentially, how best it can be used to benefit mankind's progression towards his ultimate destiny, that of becoming conquerors of all existence. I will prove to my colleagues that not only have I fully recovered from my past sickness but that my recovery is so complete that in comparison to me, it is they who are sick; they will look upon me with envy. I will be awarded the most prestigious academic prizes. The American government will pay me vast sums to access the results of my research. I will use my extraordinary wealth to purchase a better home and a better car and anything else I desire. And then...'

Arthur glanced at his watch. It was long past the time that Molly was due to arrive home from work.

'And then I will get myself a better wife,' Arthur said. 'And then, when I have proven my superiority to everyone and everything, when I have conquered everything there is to conquer...'

Arthur suddenly felt overwhelmingly depressed. Exhausted by the feeling, he slowly stood up, then slowly walked out of the living room, through the hallway and into the bedroom. He sat on the edge of the bed and slowly removed his shoes and socks, his brown corduroy jacket and trousers, his brown necktie, his shirt and his underpants, then lay on the bed. The whole of his body was still sunburnt bright red. He closed his eyes but could not sleep.

'And then...' he said. 'And then...'

He opened his eyes.

'It is all so pointless,' he said. 'There is no point in my living. There is no point at all. Suicide is the only rational course of action. It is the only rational course of action for anyone.'

Arthur stood up, walked out of the bedroom, through the hallway, into the kitchen, opened a drawer and removed a sharp knife.

'You must be Arthur,' said a female voice from behind him.

Arthur turned around and saw, standing in the hallway, the woman with long, white hair, dressed in her black cloak. Arthur stared at her with his mouth wide open in shock. Without hesitating, the woman deftly threw a small, white, spherical pill into Arthur's mouth and down his throat. Arthur passed out.

Arthur awoke. He was lying, naked, face up, on grass. He opened his eyes and saw a clear, starry, moonless night sky. He raised his head and recognised his surroundings as Rock Creek Cemetery.

He stood up. He was facing two graves, side by side, both filled with completely black soil.

At the end of one of the graves was a gravestone carved with the words:

The Moon

Approximately 4,500,000,000 BCE – 1969

Two grey wolves were using their front paws to dig into the grave's black soil; they were whimpering desperately.

At the end of the other grave was a gravestone carved with the words:

Molly Hart

1941-1969

Arthur began to cry.

Standing between the two graves was the woman with long, white hair, dressed in her black cloak, and holding a white shovel in her left hand. She looked at Arthur and screamed:

'You buried them alive! You buried them alive!'

Arthur stared back at the woman, then ran towards her, grabbed the white shovel and dug it into Molly's grave. He dug frantically, depositing shovelful after shovelful of the completely black soil into a pile on the grass between the two graves. He dug and dug until, from beneath the black soil in the bottom of the grave, two hands emerged and reached up into the air. Arthur threw the white shovel down, fell to his knees, took hold of the hands and pulled. From beneath the black soil, Molly emerged, sitting up and gasping in the air. Arthur cried out in relief, then quickly picked up the white shovel and turned to the second grave. The two wolves were still digging into the grave's black soil. Arthur dug the shovel into the centre of the grave, between the two wolves. The wolves stepped back, then watched intently as Arthur dug as frantically as before, depositing shovelful after shovelful of the completely black soil onto the pile on the grass between the two graves. Arthur dug deep into the dense darkness. He dug and dug until, from beneath the black soil in the bottom of the grave, there shone a faint, white light. Arthur threw the white shovel down, fell to his knees, then watched as, from beneath the black soil, the shining full moon emerged. Arthur again cried out in relief. He reached his hands towards the shining moon but it rose up out of the black soil, out of the grave and into the air before Arthur could touch it. Arthur watched the shining moon rise straight up into the clear night sky. Although the moon grew further away from Arthur, it appeared to remain the same size.

The moon ascended, higher and higher, until it reached its rightful place, then hovered, full and gently shining.

Arthur awoke. He was lying, naked, face up, on a floor. He opened his eyes and saw his kitchen ceiling. He raised his head and saw Molly standing in front of him, looking down at him with a concerned expression. Arthur sighed in relief.

'How many loves do you have, Arthur?' Molly asked.

'Two, of course,' Arthur said.

Molly smiled.

Arthur turned his head to look out of the kitchen window and saw a clear, starry night sky surrounding a shining full moon. Arthur sighed in relief again.

'Show him what he looks like,' said a female voice from behind him.

Arthur stood up and turned around. Sat at the kitchen table, wearing her black cloak, was the woman with long, white hair. Arthur turned back around to face Molly and whispered:

'Who is that?'

'A friend,' Molly whispered.

Arthur nodded, then Molly beckoned Arthur to follow her as she walked out of the kitchen and into the hallway. Arthur followed.

Molly pointed at a full-length mirror hanging on the wall and said:

'Take a look at yourself, Arthur.'

Arthur stood facing the mirror.

The right side of Arthur's body was still sunburnt bright red, but the left side of his body was now excessively pale; the bright red right side met the excessively pale left side in the middle of his body, creating a vertical boundary line down his front and back.

Arthur looked at his reflection and smiled. Then he turned around and embraced Molly.

'I am touching you!' Arthur said, tears of joy falling from his eyes. 'I am really touching you!'

'Yes, Arthur,' Molly said, also with tears of joy falling from her eyes.

Arthur and Molly let go of one another, then stood gazing at each other and smiling.

In the kitchen, the woman with long, white hair stood up, then walked into the hallway.

'Do you want to touch your other love, Arthur?' she asked.

'Yes!' said Arthur.

'I mean *really* touch her, not just land upon her. Do you want to touch her spirit and know her in her entirety?'

'Yes!' said Arthur.

'Follow me,' the woman with long, white hair said.

She walked through the hallway, towards the front door, opened it, then stepped outside. Arthur and Molly followed.

The woman with long, white hair walked towards Arthur and Molly's car. When she reached it, she turned around and said:

'Key?'

Molly removed her car key from her trouser pocket and handed it to the woman with long, white hair who opened the car door on the driver's side, sat in the driver's seat, then started the engine. Molly sat in the front passenger seat. Arthur sat in the back. As soon as all the car's doors were closed, the woman with long, white hair sped out of the drive, along the street and onto the freeway.

Approximately one hour later, the car arrived at Sandy Point. The woman with long, white hair switched off the engine, then led Arthur and Molly down to the beach.

The night sky was clear and starry and the moon was full above the ocean. The tide was out: the ocean's edge far away across the sand.

The woman with long, white hair walked towards the

ocean. Arthur and Molly followed.

When the woman with long, white hair reached the ocean's edge, she bowed down to the moon, then turned around and beckoned Molly to stand next to her. The two women stood with the waves gently lapping behind them.

The woman with long, white hair looked at Arthur and said:

'Stand facing the ocean, a few metres away from the edge.'

Arthur did so.

'Now look up at the moon.'

Arthur looked up at the shining full moon.

'Now use the sand to make a representation of the moon.'

Arthur crouched down, scooped up handfuls of the damp sand and packed them together into a pile. He then sculpted the pile into a sphere, approximately the size of an adult human head. He adjusted the shape of the sculpture to more closely resemble that of the moon by adding slight protuberances here and there. Then on the sculpture's surface, he created a series of shallow, circular indentations of various sizes to represent the largest of the moon's craters. He rendered the sculpture with as much accuracy as he could and handled the sand with as much care as he could. When he had completed the task to the best of his ability, he stepped back from the sculpture.

'Now wait,' the woman with long, white hair said.

She beckoned Molly to follow her as she walked back across the beach, away from the ocean and away from Arthur. The two women continued walking until the sand beneath their shoes was dry, then they sat down on the beach, facing the ocean.

Far in front of them, Arthur stood, alone and naked, his right side sunburnt bright red and his left side excessively pale, facing his sand sculpture of the moon, which sat on the beach between him and the ocean, gently illuminated by the real full moon above.

He waited.

Slowly, the ocean grew closer to the sand sculpture; it grew closer and closer, until it was lapping against it. Then the sand sculpture collapsed and disintegrated. The moon had caused the tide to come in, destroying the representation of itself.

Arthur looked up in wonder at the gently shining mystery hovering in the dark sky above, and with tears of joy falling from his eyes, said:

'What is that?'

Discover more Mike Russell books
at www.strangebooks.com

Printed in Great Britain
by Amazon